T4-AKX-684

This Book Belongs To:

....

Intrepid Adventurer

Published by Arete LLC

Copyright © 2013 Arete LLC

All rights reserved. No part of this book may be reproduced
or utilized in any form or by any means, electronic or
mechanical, including photocopying, recording or otherwise,
without the written permission of the publisher.

Phew! Enough of the legal mumbo jumbo! This incredible
adventure is brought to you by the people at Zylie & Friends,
founded by the mother and son team of Mary Beth Minton
and Matt McCarty. For us, every day is an adventure, and we
hope you'll join us!

adventure with style and a smile

Visit us at www.zyliethebear.com
or email questions@zyliethebear.com

or write to us:
Zylie & Friends, Arete LLC, PO Box 30157, New York, NY 10011
Zylie™ is a trademark of Arete LLC

Book design by Alissa Faden

ISBN 978-0-9889066-2-4

Printed in China

Zylie's

ADVENTURE
ON THE
SILK ROAD

Written by **Kathy Pilon**

Illustrated by
Matt Slepitza

ZYLIE & FRIENDS | NEW YORK

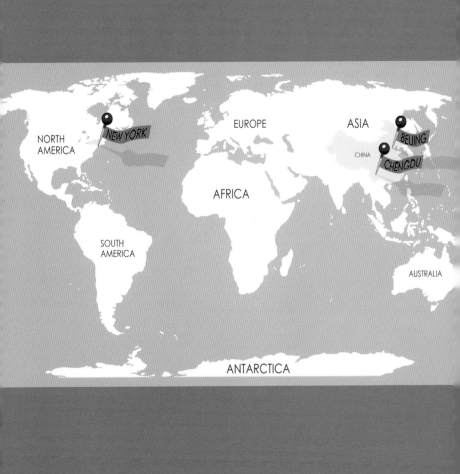

Hi, I'm Zylie!

You may not know me, but I've been on quite a journey! Actually my Aunt Willa would call it an adventure. I am a young bear from Manhattan and I live with my little brother Theo, who is always sneezing and getting into trouble.

Theo and I live with my Aunt Willa in her apartment on Park Avenue. We had a really exciting adventure in the "Big Apple," as they call it, and now Theo and I are off to China! I wonder what this story has in store for us!

Join us on this exciting adventure, and who knows where we will go from here! As my Aunt Willa says, no matter how near or far you go, every day is an adventure!

P.S. Whenever you see one of these ♀, flip to the back of the book to learn more!

BOOM! RAT-A-TAT! BOOM! RAT-A-TAT! BOOM, BOOM, BOOM!

Zylie and Theo watched the colorfully costumed band play their traditional Chinese instruments on the streets of Chengdu, China.

"Wow, this music is great!" shouted Zylie. "I've never heard anything like it before."

But Theo didn't hear a word his sister said.

Zylie was especially curious about the exotic red drum being played by a panda bear.

When the song ended, everyone in the crowd let out a great big cheer…except Theo. He was still dancing to some imaginary music in his head. It made the panda laugh.

"I guess he wasn't ready for you to stop playing," said Zylie to the drummer. "Hi! I'm Zylie, and the dancing bear here is my little brother Theo. We're visiting from New York!"

"Hi! I'm Shen. What brings you all the way over here?" asked the panda.

"Well, I wrote an essay about China for a contest and won first place," said Zylie. "And this trip was the prize!"

"That's a really cool-looking drum, Shen," said Theo.

Shen explained that the instruments are called Red Flower Drums. They were played by warriors a long time ago.

"The red drum is a symbol of power in the Chinese culture," said Shen. "I mostly just play it at special ceremonies. What I *really* wanna be is a rock star!"

Shen pounded out a loud rock 'n' roll rhythm on his drum.

"Cool! Maybe Theo and I will see you on stage one day," said Zylie.

"You can count on it!" responded Shen.

Shen invited Zylie and Theo to join him for lunch at a restaurant that served only one thing: dumplings.

"What's a dumpling?" asked Theo.

"It's a little ball of dough filled with different surprises," explained Shen. "It's delicious!"

The waitress gave each of them a set of wooden chopsticks ②. "*Kuàizi,*" said the waitress in Chinese.

"That's our word for chopsticks," said Shen. "It's pronounced like this: '*kwa-ee–tzz.*'"

"That's a real tongue-twister," Zylie said as she tried saying it out loud.

Zylie carefully lifted up a dumpling between her two chopsticks. But instead of landing in her mouth, it shot all the way across the room and hit the waitress.

"Oops! Sorry about that!" Zylie said.

"How do you say 'fork, please' in Chinese?" she asked with a laugh.

Shen showed them how to use the chopsticks. "I should probably warn you," he said as he ate a dumpling, "our food is known for its spiciness."

"Oh no! Look at the time!" said Shen, jumping up. "I've got to get moving."

"Wait," said Theo. "Don't we get fortune cookies?"

"There are no fortune cookies here," said Shen as he raced for the door. "That's an American invention, not an authentic Chinese tradition at all."

Out on the street, Zylie pulled a small piece of paper from her purse. "Well, authentic or not, I carry an old fortune with me because it has my lucky numbers on the back."

She showed it to Shen. "What does the front say?"

无论你走到哪里, 请让心跟随者你

Shen read the Chinese characters and smiled. "It's a quote from Confucius, a famous Chinese philosopher. It says, '*Wheresoever you go, go with all your heart.*'"

"I like that. It's perfect for me!" exclaimed Zylie. When she looked up, Shen was already halfway down the street.

"Well then, maybe you'd like to join me on my mission," Shen called back to her.

"Your MISSION?!" said Theo and Zylie at the same time.

They sprinted to catch up with Shen.

"It's a tradition in my village," Shen explained as he sped along. "When pandas reach my age, we go to different places throughout China and bring back something special from each one."

"So what's the big rush?" Theo panted.

"I only have two days to do it, and this is already day one!" Shen looked frantically up and down the street. "I haven't found anything yet here in Chengdu!"

Zylie gestured at the lanterns that lined all the streets in the city. "How about one of those?" she suggested. "I've read about the Lantern Festivals [3] and how they symbolize people letting go of their old selves to welcome the New Year with a fresh start."

Shen considered it. "I'm not sure a lantern will be special enough."

"Didn't someone back home tell you the kinds of things you're supposed to collect?" asked Theo.

"No," said Shen. "The whole point of the mission is that I have to figure it out for myself. Except I don't have a clue. All I know is that if I fail, I will disappoint the village elders and bring shame to my family."

"Well then," said Zylie brightly, "we'll help you. Maybe together we'll just *know* when something's special enough."

"Thanks," said Shen. "But we've got to hurry. I have to be done with my mission and back home by midnight tomorrow night. Let's catch a train!"

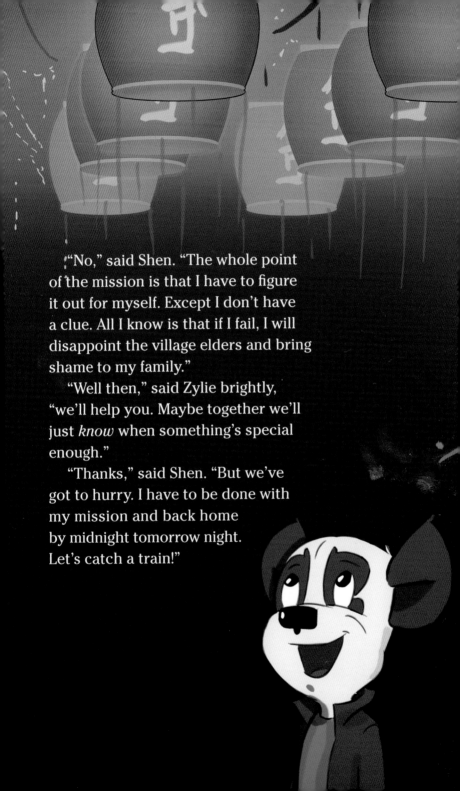

Aboard a high-speed train , Zylie looked out the window as the countryside whizzed by in a blur.

"You know, this train goes almost 200 miles an hour!" said Shen. "We'll be there in two hours."

"That means I'll have time to shop for a new outfit when we get to Xi'an⑤," said Zylie, smiling. "I need to find something special to wear for my journey around China."

"I hope I find something special too," Shen said quietly to himself.

Getting off the train, they switched to one of China's most ancient forms of transportation: a rickshaw ⑥. They took a bumpy but fun ride through the streets of Xi'an.

"Is this the famous Silk Road?" asked Theo.

The rickshaw driver explained that the Silk Road is not really a road at all.

"In the old days, any route from China to Rome was called the Silk Road," he said. "It was a 4,000-mile trip, and the city of Xi'an was the starting point."

"So why was it called the Silk Road?" asked Zylie.

"Although people traded lots of things along the route," the driver explained, "silk was the most rare, and people would travel great distances for it."

"People like me!" exclaimed Zylie as they pulled up to a clothing boutique. "I see a silk dress with my name on it. Thanks for the lift!"

"This is perfect," said Zylie as she modeled a red dress for the others. "But I love the green one too. Hmm, decisions, decisions."

"You look gorgeous," said the shop owner. "They're both beautiful on you."

"Thank you," beamed Zylie. "Then I've made my choice. I'll take the green...AND the red."

Before they left the clothing boutique, the shop owner gave each of them a silk handkerchief to remember their time in Xi'an.

"Finally! My first special thing!" shouted Shen happily.

They gave high fives to each other as they headed toward two majestic towers in the center of the city.

"The Bell Tower and Drum Tower ⑦ of Xi'an were built more than 600 years ago," said Shen.

"Wow!" Theo said, amazed. "That's even older than Aunt Willa!" Zylie and Shen burst out laughing.

"I wrote about these towers in my essay," said Zylie. "Xi'an was the capital of China in ancient times. These towers were built exactly in the center of town so they could easily see if enemies were coming from any direction."

Shen pulled his drumsticks out of his backpack and started beating on the biggest drum he'd ever seen.

Zylie happily snapped a picture of him on her ZyPhone. "Now that's a great memento!" she said happily.

"HE-YAAAA!" A loud yell got Zylie's attention as they left the tower.

"It's a martial arts demonstration," she said. They all ran over to watch just as the Master splintered a thick block of wood with his bare hands.

For fun, Shen imitated the yell and chopping motion they had just witnessed. He had no idea he was being watched.

"Ah, we have a volunteer from the audience," said the Master. He was staring right at Shen.

"Who, me?" squeaked Shen. He mustered up some courage. "Okay...sure. Why not?"

Before he knew it, Shen had been flipped, spun, rolled, kicked, tripped and tossed onto a soft mat. Then the Master showed Shen how to do the flipping himself. When he successfully threw the Master to the ground, the audience burst into applause.

Shen and the Master bowed to one another. "You are a brave young man, Mr. Shen," said the Master. "Take this bell and carry it with you always. It will protect you from harm."

"Thank you, sir!" said Shen excitedly, handing the bell to Theo to hold. "Now I have something really special to show you!"

"I can't believe I'm about to see the Terracotta Warriors ⑧ with my own eyes!" said Zylie.

"The terra-whoozie-whatzies?" asked Theo. "What are you talking about?"

"Look, right there," said Zylie. She gestured to a large pit filled with thousands of life-size clay statues.

"Awesome – it's an entire army!" exclaimed Theo.

Shen translated from a museum pamphlet. "This is the tomb of the first Emperor of China. He was buried with thousands of clay statues to protect him in the afterlife. These soldiers, horses and chariots are over 2,000 years old!"

"Wow, Theo, what do you think of that?" asked Zylie, looking around.

There was no answer.
Theo was gone!

"Theo! Theo!" Zylie and Shen ran all through the museum looking for him. "He has to be here somewhere," said Zylie nervously.

Suddenly Shen stopped. "Listen," he said. "Do you hear that ringing? Let's follow the sound."

Sure enough, there at the bottom of a pit sat Theo, ringing the bell from the Master.

"Help me!" he yelled. "I fell in."

Shen pulled Theo out of the pit. "That was a smart idea to ring the bell," he told Theo. "I guess the Master was right. It kept you safe from harm."

"Yeah," said Theo. "But I think I'm allergic to clay. Ah-CHOO!"

The three boarded another high-speed train to their next destination. This time they stayed in a special sleeping compartment.

Theo's loud snoring woke Zylie up in the middle of the night. She saw Shen staring out the window, looking worried. "I haven't gathered enough special things yet," Shen told Zylie.

"It's all going to be OK, Shen," Zylie said. She tried getting his mind off his mission. "Hey, is it true that fireworks were first invented in China right near your village?"

Shen brightened. "It is true. In fact, if I successfully complete my mission, I'll be honored with a big fireworks display tomorrow night in front of the whole village," Shen said. "But if I fail...I will disappoint everyone."

Just then Theo let out a big snore. He rolled right out of his bunk bed and landed on the floor with a thud.

"Ouch!" cried Theo. "Hey, are we there yet? And where are we going, anyway?"

"It's a surprise," said Shen.

"The Great Wall of China . Wow, it's huge!" said Zylie, her eyes wide with wonder.

"I wish I had my skateboard with me," said Theo. "I could ride forever."

"Well, don't get any of your crazy ideas. I don't feel like chasing you for 5,500 miles," warned Zylie.

Suddenly a dragon appeared in the sky, heading straight for them!

"Watch out!" shouted Theo.

The dragon swooped right past them.

"It's just a kite," laughed Shen. "They were invented here in China over 3,000 years ago."

"Look! It's come loose from its string!" shouted Theo as he jumped up to catch it.

"Thank you for saving my kite," shouted a man running toward them.

As Theo handed the kite to the man, he smiled and said, "No. You keep it as my gift."

"I have an idea," said Theo, handing the kite to Shen. "Now you have another special gift!"

Later, they were in the center of China's capital, Beijing .

Shen pointed to a big red building with a large gate. "And that is the entrance to the Forbidden City ⑪."

"Forbidden City?" said Theo. "What's forbidden about it?"

"Well, since it used to be the palace where the emperors and their royal families lived," explained Shen, "it was forbidden to commoners, like us!"

"Can we go in there now?" asked Zylie.

"Sure," Shen answered. "That was a long time ago. Now it's a museum."

"Then let's go!" said Zylie, super excited.

"Hold it!" said Theo.   "What's going on over there?"

A crowd had gathered to help a famous chef attempt to make the world's longest noodle.

"He's trying to roll a noodle that's over one mile long," said one of the assistants. "Come on, he needs everyone's help!"

Zylie, Theo and Shen found themselves pulling and stretching a piece of rice noodle. When they were done, it was official: a new world record of 1,800 meters.

Zylie quickly calculated the length on her ZyPhone. "That's 1.1 miles," she said, elated.

"Thank you for your help," said the chef. "Here, try some for yourselves. You deserve it."

Theo put one end of it in his mouth and sucked it up with one giant slurp. Zylie slowly chewed on her piece, while Shen stuck his in a pocket for later.

The three walked through the giant gate of the Forbidden City. They crossed a bridge and noticed lots of beautiful lotus flowers floating on the water below.

"It says here that if you throw a coin and it lands inside one of the flowers, your wish will come true," said Zylie. "Let's try it."

All three of them made a wish and threw their coins. Shen's coin was the only one that landed in a flower.

"What did you wish for?" Zylie asked Shen.

"I wished for more adventures with you and Theo."

"Well, then I'm glad yours is the wish that will come true!" said Zylie.

After exploring the Forbidden City, they ran to catch a train to get back to Shen's village before midnight.

Once on board, Shen pulled out his list of special gifts. "Oh no!" he cried out. "I didn't bring anything back from Beijing."

"Don't you still have your noodle?" asked Theo.

Shen reached into his pocket and pulled out his piece of the world's longest noodle. "Theo, you're a genius!"

Shen stored the noodle safely in his backpack and wrote it down on his list.

The train pulled into the village station just a few minutes before midnight. They raced into the town square with just seconds to spare.

Shen bowed before the village elders. His grandfather spoke. "Young Shen, please share with us what transpired on your mission."

Shen excitedly told them the highlights of his adventure, delighting the crowd with all the amazing stories of his journey.

"And now, here are the special things that I've brought back," Shen said proudly.

He reached into his
backpack, but...
it was empty!

"Oh no!" he cried.
"Everything must've fallen
out of it on the train!" Shen
instantly realized what this
meant.

"I'm so sorry... I've let you
all down. I have failed." Shen
dropped his head in shame.

His grandfather looked at him
in silence for a long time, and then
nodded his head.

Suddenly, the sky lit up with explosions of color.

"Fireworks!" said Zylie. "Shen, you did it. You completed your mission!" The whole village was cheering.

Shen's smile went from ear to ear. He gave Zylie and Theo each a giant bear hug. "I couldn't have done it without you! Come on, let's celebrate!"

Shen looked up. "But Grandfather, I don't understand. I failed. I didn't bring back anything special."

His grandfather smiled. "No, Shen, just the opposite is true," he said. "From your journey you have brought back the most special thing of all...wonderful memories. They are extraordinary treasures that you can hold in your heart and mind forever. There is nothing more special in all the world."

Just then, Zylie's ZyPhone buzzed. It was an email. "Hey, it's from Aunt Willa. She's in Australia and wants us to meet her there tomorrow," said Zylie.

"Australia? I've always wanted to go there," said Shen, looking a little sad.

"Why don't you come *with* us, Shen?" Zylie suggested. "We'll have another great adventure together. Your lotus flower wish will come true!"

Shen's eyes lit up. "Can I, Grandfather? Please?"

Shen's grandfather considered his request. "But what about your studies?" he asked.

Zylie knew she had to say something to help. "When I was researching my essay, I remember a Chinese proverb that said: '*It is better to travel ten thousand miles than to read ten thousand books.*'"

Grandfather smiled and put his arm around Shen. "You have chosen your friends well," he said. "Zylie speaks very wisely."

"Does that mean I can go?" said Shen hopefully.

"Yes. But only on one condition," said Grandfather.

"What?" asked Shen. "Anything!"

"Promise you will bring back something *special*," Grandfather said with a wink.

Everyone laughed and they celebrated through the night.

Follow more of Zylie's adventures
online at www.zyliethebear.com/passport.

And did you know that Zylie and Shen exist not only
as lovable characters in our stories, but also as award-
winning 18" jointed plush animals? They do! They even
come complete with fashionable outfits, accessories
and, most importantly for their travels, their passports.

Each passport has a unique code on the back, which
you can use to log in and unlock exclusive new content,
stories and adventures! Zylie's adventures never end, so
be sure to check back often!

Flip the page to check out the Spotlight and Glossary
sections to learn more about some of the terms you saw
in this adventure.

We hope you enjoyed the story!

Cheers,

Team Zylie

SPOTLIGHT

1. Chengdu is a major city located in central China. It is home of the Wolong National Nature Reserve, a protected area for giant pandas. Pandas are among the rarest animals in the world and need protection in order to live.

2. In China, these long narrow sticks have been used as eating utensils to pick up food for over 3,000 years and are still used today.

3. This festival is celebrated in various parts of the world on the last day of the Lunar New Year. In China, it officially ends the Chinese New Year celebrations.

4. The rail system in China is one of the largest in the world. High-speed trains were introduced in 2007, making travel in this very large country easier and faster. The high-speed trains can travel over 200 miles per hour.

5. Located in central northwest China, Xi'an is one of the oldest cities in the world and is considered to be the root of Chinese civilization. It was the capital of China for almost 2,000 years.

6. These two-wheeled passenger carts are human-powered. Some are pulled by a person, and others are pulled by someone on a bicycle.

7. In ancient China, every city had a drum tower and a bell tower, which were used to keep time. The bell was rung at dawn each day and the drum at dusk. The bell and drum towers in Xi'an were built more than 600 years ago and are among the most beautiful and best-preserved in the country. They stand at the center of the city, providing a good view of the surrounding countryside.

8. Terracotta is a brownish-red clay. In 1974, farmers digging a well in Xi'an discovered by chance a 2,000-year-old pit filled with life-size clay soldiers. Scientists eventually uncovered almost 8,000 different statues including horses, chariots and an entire army. China's first emperor had the statues built and buried with him in his tomb to protect him in the afterlife. The Terracotta Warrior and Horse Museum was built over the pit where they were found.

9. Long ago, many parts of China had walls around their borders for protection, but the Great Wall was started by the first emperor of China over 2,000 years ago. He used some of the existing walls and added to them. Over the years, many other emperors continued adding to it, making it 5,500 miles long!

10. One of the largest cities in the world, Beijing is the capital of the People's Republic of China.

11. Built in 1406, the Forbidden City was the Chinese Imperial Palace until 1911. During a span of more than 500 years, it was the home of 24 different emperors and their households, and served as the political center of the Chinese government. It is located in the center of Beijing and now houses the Palace Museum.

GLOSSARY

Afterlife
Refers to the time after a person dies. Many cultures believe that a person's spirit continues to live in some form after death on earth.

Allergy
A body's reaction to something it doesn't like. Allergies can cause a runny nose, itchy eyes and lots of sneezes.

Ancient
From olden times.

Authentic
Genuine or real. Not fake or an imitation.

Chariot
A two-wheeled horse-drawn vehicle of ancient times used in battle.

Culture
The behaviors and beliefs common to a country.

Destination
A place to which someone is making a journey.

Elders
Important people in a community, often older and wiser.

Emperor
A male supreme ruler of a country.

Exotic
Unusual or different.

Forbidden
Not permitted or allowed.

Handkerchief
A small piece of cloth, usually used for wiping one's nose, eyes or face.

Invent
To create something that didn't exist before.

Majestic
In a grand style.

Mission
A special assignment given to a person or a group.

Palace
The home of a king, queen or emperor, usually very large and grand.

Philosopher
A person who offers views or theories on important ideas.

Proverb
A wise saying that easily expresses a truth or commonly held belief.

Silk
Soft, beautiful fabric made from the cocoon of the silkworm, originally found only in China.

Solo
A thing done by one person alone, unaccompanied.

Symbol
Something that stands for or suggests something else, often a visible sign of something invisible.

Tradition
A way of acting or thinking that is handed down from parents to children over many, many years in a culture.

Transpire
To happen or occur; take place.

Village
A small community, usually in the countryside.

Warrior
Soldier.

ZyPhone
Zylie's very own phone with a camera and her music; something she takes with her everywhere.

WHERE DO YOU THINK ZYLIE WILL GO NEXT?

Use this blank page to write your own adventure!